MW01227832

Grizzly Plot

By
Gretchen S.B.

For information contact :
GretchenS.B.author@gmail.com
http://www.GretchenSB.com

Book and Cover design by Designer

Acknowledgments

Thank you to my editor Ayden at WhalesEdits. You made this book readable for everyone.

Thank you to the folks at Get Covers for giving this book such a beautiful cover.

As always, thank you to my friends and family who cheer me on as I work toward my dream of being a full-time author.

Last of all, but not least, is the Hubster. Although he hates to be mentioned, he deserves credit for all his support.

Chapter 1

Patrick

"I don't care how you feel about it, Patrick! We are getting you some kind of security system," his uncle Peter announced harshly.

"Did you two old men con me in to helping you with a Costco run when we are really here getting a security system that I have said repeatedly I don't want?" Patrick answered pointedly, glaring between his father and uncle.

His father shrugged. "Your mother did want me to pick up some things while we were here." He pulled out a crumpled slip of paper from his jacket pocket.

Uncle Peter narrowed his eyes at his brother. "Alexander focus!"

His father shrugged and slid the paper back into his pocket. "I learned long ago Beth is a force to be reckoned with from Halloween to New Year's. I am not about to get in the way of that...again."

Frowning at his younger brother, Uncle Peter sighed before turning back to Patrick. "Look, you need some kind of alarm or camera, if only so we can see who's leaving notes on your property."

"It's wolves."

His uncle gave him a hard stare. "We need to know which wolves so we can bring it to Sullivan and Mark."

Sullivan and Mark were the alpha and beta for the Forest's Edge pack. These notes started appearing in his mail slot a week ago after Patrick and his brother, Ollie, helped Mark fend off a group of wolf shifters, hoping to overthrow the pack hierarchy.

So far, only Patrick had received notes, which he was grateful for—Ollie had a brand-new mate and was hypervigilant about protecting her. Patrick didn't know how his usually calm older brother would react if people left threats anywhere near Elsie.

"Fine, camera only. I don't want lights going off in the backyard every time Sprinkles goes out to pee. It will scare the crap out of her and me."

"Maybe that's the point," his uncle muttered as they started walking, presumably to the aisle that held security equipment.

Sprinkles was a Shiba Inu-boxer mix Patrick had inherited from one of his good friends. His friend's little girl adored Sprinkles, but it became clear his son was allergic. His friend's daughter used some kind of little girl magic on Patrick, and he ended up Sprinkles's new owner. That was three years ago.

"If I let you install cameras, will you stop bothering me about an alarm system?" Patrick huffed.

His uncle eyed him for a moment, his expression fluctuating between suspicious and agitated.

"Oh, she will definitely want one of these," his father exclaimed before briskly wandering off two aisles down.

With an exasperated sigh, Peter lifted his hands, then let them fall slack by his sides. "Fine, if you at least let us install cameras in the front, back, one on each side, I will drop the issue for now. And motion sensers we can program to only register above Sprinkles's height. Once Sullivan and Mark have the pictures, they can discipline the culprits accordingly."

"You know they're only going to discipline them because Ollie and Mark's mates are sisters." Patrick raised his eyebrow at his uncle, waiting for the older man to challenge his statement.

Though the population of Forest's Edge was mainly supernatural, and for that they were grateful, there still wasn't anything beyond polite conversation between the different species.

His uncle muttered something Patrick couldn't quite hear, turning away and heading towards the security cameras.

Not that Patrick would ever admit it to his father or his uncle, but he was actually getting a little agitated with the notes being left in his mail slot. They were always done in serial killer handwriting and always just shy of threatening. The last one said, *Keep that bear snout out of wolf business.* He honestly didn't know why he was still getting notes, as the only wolf business he had been involved in was helping his brother Ollie defend his mate when a group of drunk werewolves attacked Mark at their house.

The sooner he could be done with this nonsense, the sooner he could get back to his regular schedule. He found himself coming home and taking his lunch at odd times during the day in hopes of catching whoever was leaving these notes. But so far, Patrick had seen no one.

"Where the hell did your father wander off to? He is supposed to be giving his opinion on which one we should use," his uncle asked frustratedly.

Patrick couldn't help but smirk. He knew what his father was doing. His human mother loved holidays, and his father indulged her completely. While the rest of the year his father was more grizzly bear than man, holiday season was different, and he loved putting that joyous smile on his mate's face. Patrick knew they were not going to see his father again until he collected everything on whatever list his mom had given him.

"Yeah, he's gone Uncle Peter. It's better if we just call him when we're ready to leave."

His uncle grumbled under his breath again before he returned to comparing the cameras.

Chapter 2

Four Days Earlier
Melody

Melody frowned when she heard male voices coming from the kitchen of her apartment, which she shared with her big brother, Harrison. Melody had gone to a friend's Thanksgiving in Seattle, then made it a mini vacation while she revisited her college stomping grounds with friends. The last thing she wanted to deal with after a long car ride was visitors.

She dropped her bag at the end of the entryway and turned to the left to peek into a small kitchen and living room space.

Inwardly, she groaned when she saw Harrison sitting at the kitchen table with two of their idiot cousins, Mick and Bruce. The two of them thought they were tough and had big plans for themselves. In actuality, they never thought through any of their actions and weren't as strong as they imagined they were. They had been mumbling about fighting their way up the ranks of the Wolfpack for years, but they never managed anything real. Their whining had gotten worse since the pack beta was overthrown about six months ago.

Melody wasn't a member of the pack. She made an agreement with its current alpha that she didn't have to abide by any pack rules, but she wouldn't make a nuisance of herself. They wouldn't have her back if something went wrong, but she didn't have to deal with any of the nonsense and politics that came with being part of the pack. Her brother, on the other hand, liked that kind of thing.

She scanned the three of them as they finally noticed her presence. The looks on their faces made her nervous, and dread seeped through the lining of her stomach. "What did you idiots do?" she asked as she threw her hands up on her hips and scowled.

"What makes you think we did anything?" Bruce snaps back.

"Harrison?" she demanded, raising an eyebrow at him.

Her brother exchanged wary looks with her before his eyes drifted back to their cousins. "They, along with some cousins on the other side of their family, apparently wanted to teach the new beta a lesson about knowing his place."

Melody didn't have to hear the rest to know the crap heading their way. Slowly, she shut her eyes and lowered her head.

"Please tell me you are not on the run and hiding out here?"

Both her cousins shouted, "No!" indignantly.

"They just got released today. They've been in jail for several days until it was decided no one was going to press charges. But for obvious reasons, the alpha and beta are not happy."

"You don't say?" she snipped sarcastically. She threw up her hands and pointed an angry finger at all three of them.

"I don't want anything to do with this, which means I want you out of my apartment. I don't want to be seen as an accomplice to any of your shenanigans." She directed her gaze and finger at her brother. "You shouldn't either. Now I'm going to unpack. By the time I'm done, I want you two gone or I'm gonna start raising hell."

She turned and went walking back the way she came. Though she heard snarls over her shoulder, she knew her cousins would leave without a fight. First, Harrison would always support her over them. Second, Melody had beaten them bloody in fights since they were teenagers. While Melody chose not to be a part of the pack, she had a very dominant wolf, making her much stronger in every sense of the word. It was another reason she hated pack hierarchy. It itched to have someone telling her what to do.

Grabbing her bag, she stormed towards her bedroom, in the opposite direction of the kitchen. She wondered what would have happened if she hadn't come back from Seattle today. Would the cousins have tried to loop Harrison into something stupid?

Sighing as she shut her bedroom door, Melody threw the duffel on the chest at the foot of her bed. She turned to Larry, her childhood teddy bear, a bit worse for wear, but she still loved him.

"Larry, I swear, I do not understand how my family could be so stupid."

Larry, of course, kept his wisdom to himself. Not that she expected any different.

She heard the front door open and shut. A couple minutes later, there was a knock at her bedroom door.

"Come on in, Harrison."

The door creaked before she felt her brother's presence get closer.

"I wasn't going to get involved in their mess. They were coming to tell me about it and see if I would be willing to help them out. I don't know what they wanted me to do, though. You came in before they could really explain. You would think going to jail would deter them from whatever their plan was, but apparently not. I am just trying to decide if I should bring it up to the alpha or if I should let it lie." The wavering in his voice showed that Harrison was torn between betraying their cousins and being loyal to his pack.

"They didn't tell you what the plan was. So, all you'd be telling the alpha is they have a plan, something more than attacking the beta. What can he possibly do with that information?" She didn't bother to turn around and just kept unpacking the duffel bag, throwing clothes into her hamper.

"You're right, I just, I don't want something bad to happen that I could've prevented if I'd shared what I knew."

Now she saw where this was going. She slumped her shoulders, rolled her neck, and finally turned to look at her older brother. "You want to look into what those knuckleheads are doing, so you can either sabotage or report it to the alpha?"

Harrison shuffled between one foot and the other. "Yeah kinda."

"And I suppose you want me to help you?"

He simply nodded.

The two of them were inseparable when they were little, then drifted like teenagers do. But as adults, even though they were four years apart, she and her brother would never leave the other hanging. If her brother was determined to figure out what was going on, she wasn't sure she had it in her to leave him on his own. She didn't like the idea of him endangering himself to stop some weird plot their cousins had come up with.

"Okay, so what is it exactly you want to do?"

He let out a breath and smiled at her. "Well, first, let you unpack and take a post-driving nap. Then, I say we head out to the Watering Hole and see what we can hear."

The Watering Hole was a dive bar, predominantly a wolf shifter bar. While the occasional humans slipped in when they just happened by, most Forest's Edge residents stayed out of it. Other supernaturals just weren't comfortable around that many werewolves, all at once. She was sure it had something to do with how temperamental wolves could be.

"All right, sounds like a plan."

His smile widened as he nodded before backing out of the room and shutting the door behind him. Sighing again, she cracked her neck before she continued unpacking, then did exactly what her brother knew she would do, flopped down on the bed for a nap.

Chapter 3

Melody

As she and Harrison found a far table close to the dance floor, Melody was reminded of why she didn't like coming to the Watering Hole. When she was in her early twenties or home visiting from college, she liked the seedy aspect. It made her feel edgy. But now, she felt like the customers were trying too hard to maintain the aesthetic. But she was probably just jaded.

At thirty, she spent the last seven years working in cybersecurity with all kinds of unpleasant personalities. So, she might just have a more pessimistic outlook on life these days.

But then she looked over Harrison's shoulder and saw two wolf shifters in motorcycle gear practically grinding on each other on the dance floor, and she knew it was just the place, not all of Earth, she had a problem with.

"You getting anything, Mel?" her brother asked.

Melody flushed and took a long pull from her beer bottle. She actually hadn't been paying attention. Instead, she'd been judgmental and circling her own thoughts. She was supposed to be here to help her brother, not be a stuck up shewolf.

She shook her head and listened in earnest. Both Melody and Harrison had excellent hearing, better than most wolf shifters she met.

As she scanned the conversations in the room, there wasn't anything too interesting. There was some gossip, one couple fighting, one man describing some very obscene acts to the woman across the booth from him. A couple of guys at the bar talking about the stock market. Then finally, as she turned her head as if stretching, she spotted one of the cousins on Bruce's other side of the family sitting in a booth with a couple of other guys, frowning. Concentrating, she focused as much as she could on their conversation, drowning out everything else. She tried to sit as natural as possible while straining to hear, even though it meant being turned away from her brother, which anyone who paid attention would find a little weird.

"He won the beta fight fair and square," one of the guys with his back to her said.

"He shouldn't have overthrown the pack hierarchy within six months of arrival. He should've respected the pack enough to get a lay of the land first," replied the clearly drunk cousin.

"And what exactly are you wanting to do about it?"

"We need to act strategically, a pack leader that would let him do that clearly doesn't have his pack's best interest at heart," responded a man she didn't know, sitting next to the cousin.

All four men leaned in, and she had to strain to hear the next sentence. "Are you saying you want to overthrow the alpha? You think you have the strength to do that?"

The cousin straightened as if offended. "Not in a fair fight, no, but if we work together, or work as one unit like a true pack should, we can boot him, his brand-new beta, and the two lieutenants as well and start over from scratch. We need a pack hierarchy more centered on the pack that wouldn't let an interloper just step in and cut in front of more deserving wolves who know the pack, who put in their time in the hierarchy.

"It's very unsteady reasoning. Pack positions have always been given to the best fighter. Why are you suggesting we change that now?"

"Because," the cousin shouted as he pounded on the table, and several people turned in their direction. He lowered his voice after that, but anyone listening would still hear him if they tried.

"Not only did he let some new guy take over with no pack loyalty or history, but Sullivan has also been tightening the rains on how we, as wolf shifters, should act. Our cousin Bruce and Scales got into a fight in an alley, and some random bear shifter broke it up. Had the audacity to call the sheriff. The sheriff dragged them into jail, and when the alpha was called on their behalf, Sullivan said they could stay in overnight. Some bullshit about 'If they were going to be partially shifting out in the open where humans could see them, they could deal with the consequences.' He didn't come to his pack's defense. It's not as if there were humans around. We should be running this city, and running humans out of it. Not hiding like we have to almost everywhere else in the world."

He was getting louder now and drawing more attention. The man next to him elbowed him and whispered something. Then, they all started speaking quietly and Melody couldn't make it out.

She turned to her brother and gave him a wary look. "Did you hear any of that?" she whispered.

"Only the end after he pounded on the table, but that was enough to know the direction they were going. Am I right in piecing together that they want a hostile takeover of some kind?" His eyes were a little wide and worried. Clearly hoping his sister would correct him.

Unfortunately, she couldn't, so she just nodded.

"Dammit, I don't think bar talk is enough to go to Sullivan with." He looked at her as if asking her opinion.

She just shrugged. "I don't have anything to do with the pack. Remember, I haven't been a party to pack politics since I was twenty-three. And when I was, it was a different alpha."

Harrison slumped his shoulders. "Crap, let's finish our beers and get outta here. I need to think. I don't know what the best way to handle this is." He chugged the rest of his beer.

Melody did the same before the two of them rose and strode out of the bar as casually as they could manage.

Once they were out in the brisk November air, she took a deep breath. "I don't think we should get involved in this, Harrison. I know what you're thinking—that you should get close to the cousins and find out exactly what they're doing—but you shouldn't. You should just leave it alone. I don't want you to endanger yourself trying to prevent a few idiots from doing something idiotic. You're the only family I have left, that I care about anyway. I don't want to lose you to being noble and stupid." She elbowed him.

He smiled down at her indulgently. "I love you too, little sis."

The silence between them was heavy, both knowing they stumbled upon something with consequences whether they liked it or not, and neither of them having any idea what to do about it—or at least an idea they were comfortable with.

Chapter 4

Present Day
Patrick

Light flooded Patrick's bedroom, and he shot up in bed.

"What the hell?"

Sprinkles started barking from her little fuzzy bed in the corner of the room.

"Yeah, I know, I am up now too."

His large bedroom windows faced the back of the house—something that was usually a positive. But ever since two days ago when his uncle installed motion sensor lights at the back of the house, he had been anxiously waiting for them to go off in the middle the night. And now they had.

Springing out of bed, he pulled back the curtain at the corner of the window. All he saw was his empty backyard. From the second floor, he could see slightly over the fence. Someone could crouch down close to it and be in the dark at an angle he couldn't see, but he would notice someone standing upright or walking a yard away from the fence line. There was nothing, no people, no rabbits, not even a raccoon.

"Please tell me Peter didn't install it wrong, and now it's just going to go off at random," Patrick groaned to himself as he dug around his dresser, grabbed a pair of boxer shorts, slid them on, and made his way downstairs. Even though he didn't see anything, that didn't mean he wouldn't smell anything.

While a bear shifter didn't have as strong a nose as a wolf or feline shifter, it was still good enough to differentiate scents if something had been in the backyard in the last hour or so. By the time he opened the sliding glass door, the motion sensor lights had shut themselves off. He knew he could stand about halfway onto his deck without the motion sensor registering him, so he did just that, not wanting to blind himself in case the perpetrator really was out there.

He closed the door behind him, and he could hear Sprinkles pawing at the glass door. If there was trouble, he certainly wasn't going to let his feisty dog get pummeled. She might think she's tough, but she was a princess.

Patrick closed his eyes and inhaled deeply, letting all the smells of the backyard fill his lungs. There was something, something that wasn't usually in the backyard. It smelled like salt water at a beach. It was soothing but out of place.

Frowning, he scanned the backyard again, then took his chances and stepped forward, setting off the lights, which in turn made Sprinkles bark some more. He moved, sniffed, and followed the scent to the fence line, the back right corner. It was stronger there, with a distinct scent of a shifter about it. If a shifter knew what they were looking for, there was always an identifying scent for shifters and humans. There had been a shifter he didn't know in his backyard, who climbed over the fence before he'd seen them. Growling deeply, he clenched his hands into fists as he stormed back to the house. He booted up his laptop so he could log in to the security system and watch the surveillance video.

What he saw bothered him. Whoever the shifter was, they had been in his yard for at least ten minutes. He scrolled back and watched the night vision as the shifter leapt over the side of the fence closest to the house. He couldn't really see them jumping, it being almost out of range for the camera, just limbs as they made it over the fence. They then slinked low and hugged the house. The cameras picked them up there, but the motion sensors didn't. Patrick frowned and reevaluated the system they had in place.

He could tell the shifter was female. She was in dark pants and what looked like a motorcycle jacket as she crept close to his sliding glass door.

His heart beat faster as he watched her bend down and grab something near the edge of the door before sliding into her jacket pocket and moving away again. She stiffened; the top of her body made a kind of jerking motion as if she was cursing. Then she looked up at the house, scowled, and bolted across the yard over the fence, setting off the motion sensor lights.

"What were you doing by the door?"

He watched the video again, and she clearly removed something, but he went back outside with a flashlight and examined the area around the door. There was nothing there, not even stickiness from tape or something to that effect. Scowling, he went back inside, fairly certain he wasn't going to get anymore sleep, which was a shame since it was only two in the morning. So, instead of trying to toss and turn, he decided to watch something mindless and hope it lulled him to sleep. In the morning, he'd call his uncle, and they would decide whether they're going to send that footage to Mark and his alpha or not.

A small part of him didn't want to, which was absolutely ridiculous. This person had broken into his backyard, but it didn't look like she'd done anything destructive. Then there was her scent. He loved it, never smelled anything so pleasant. It made him wonder what she would smell like in person. It made him want to roll in it, which was absurd. But then, this whole situation had been absurd from the get-go. Flopping on the couch, he turned on the TV and hoped his mind could stop reeling.

Chapter 5

Patrick

"What is she doing?" Alpha Sullivan asked as he frowned down at Patrick's laptop.

They were watching the footage from his night vision camera for the second time. When Patrick told his Uncle Peter about it, his uncle demanded they head to the alpha's house. So here they were at the alpha's house before breakfast with Sullivan and Mark.

"We can't figure it out. We also don't know what spooked her enough that she ran over the fence and set off the lights." Peter responded.

"I got curious early this morning and looked up the same times on the other cameras, but it was just a couple of trucks driving down the street around that time. I can't imagine that a couple of trucks in the front of the house spooked her that much." As he said it, Patrick knew he didn't sound convinced. The trucks very well could have been what spooked her.

"Did you get a good look at them? Like the people in the trucks or license plates?" Mark asked.

Shaking his head, Patrick paused the recording again, just after the shifter bounded over the fence. "No, they're just two dark-colored trucks you see going down the street. If it was daylight, we might have gotten a partial plate, but not at night."

"I don't like this," Mark commented. "There were no female shifters involved when my family and I were attacked. What are the odds they've recruited more people to whatever their cause is? Because I can't imagine this is unrelated."

The alpha looked from Mark to the computer and to Mark again, frowning deeply and seeming to be wading through several ideas. Finally, he shook his head and took a step back from the computer.

"I don't know, but I think I know who that is in the video. If I'm right, we can't help you. But you should be able to help yourself."

"What the hell does that mean?" his uncle growled.

The alpha shrugged, immune to Peter's anger. "Not all wolf shifters in Forest's Edge belong to the pack. I would say eighty percent. And of those last twenty percent, most are male or families who owe their loyalty to other packs. If this is who I think it is, she doesn't belong to the pack. It is therefore not our responsibility, and therefore, we can't punish her. But that also means we can't come to her defense should you want to take matters into your own hands."

Patrick did not like the sound of that at all. Not only did he not know there were wolves not beholden to the pack living in Forest's Edge, but he almost felt bad for the woman in the video. She would have no one backing her up if something happened.

"What's her name?" asked Peter, his voice deadly calm.

Sullivan rolled his shoulders back, in an effort to showcase his alpha authority. "The video isn't quite clear enough for me to say one hundred percent that it's her, so bear that in mind. I'm hesitant to give you her name in case it isn't her."

"I would know her scent. It was still lingering in the backyard, and if I smelled it again, I'd confirm her identity," Patrick interjected.

Sullivan looked at him curiously for a second, and he almost seemed to smile before his lips dropped again. "Her name is Melody Adams. Her brother Harrison is a member of my pack, but she politely asked to leave seven or eight years ago. We have an understanding that she'll stay out of our business if we stay out of hers. She is one of the more cordial packless wolves living in my territory, which is why I'm surprised to see her on this video."

Patrick narrowed his eyes at the alpha while the other man stared at the paused computer screen. Despite his words, the alpha didn't actually seem surprised. His voice was calm, bland even. Maybe he was trying not to speak ill of a former member of the pack.

"Where can we find her?" his uncle asked, folding his arms across his chest.

"I can't give you her address because she lives with her brother, and he's a pack member. So, you'll have to find a different way to hunt her down. She also works from home."

His uncle growled low and loud. He took a small step towards the alpha. Bear shifters were taller and bulkier than other shifters, so while Sullivan was large for a wolf shifter, Peter still towered over him.

"People are bothering my nephew, nearly breaking into his home, and you refuse to help us. Are you trying to cause a rift between the bear and wolf shifters, Alpha Sullivan?"

The tension in the room was so thick Patrick felt like he was choking on it. His uncle was menacing and his snarl so threatening he was surprised to see none of his uncle's body parts had shifted.

The alpha snarled back at the larger man. "My hands are tied. I cannot betray one of my pack members. I have given you her name. You can take it from there."

The two dominant shifters stared each other down for several beats before Mark stepped in between them, breaking the eye contact.

Patrick was careful to keep his tone as neutral as he could. "Well, Uncle Peter, I have to get to work. And so do you. We can work on finding this woman later."

Peter's eyes slowly shifted to him, and he watched his uncle physically rein in his anger before taking a deep breath and nodding.

He then turned to the alpha and took a step back, grabbing Patrick's laptop. "Thank you for your assistance, alpha, but if I find out there's more you could have done to help us narrow down our search, we'll be having more than words."

The alpha growled in response, but Mark put an arm on the alpha's shoulder, and the wolf's attention snapped to him instead.

Patrick cleared his throat. "Come on Uncle, let's get out of here." He snatched his laptop from his uncle's grip and started moving towards the front of the house, expecting his uncle to follow. He let out a sigh of relief when he stepped out onto the porch and his uncle was right behind him.

"There can't be many Melody Adamses in Forest's Edge. I'm sure all we have to do is ask around a couple of stores to find something," Patrick tried to soothe his uncle's anger. He wasn't entirely sure it was working.

There was a rumble as his uncle pushed in front of him and started walking down the driveway to his truck. Patrick waited a beat then followed.

"I'm gonna ask the guys at the jobsite if any of them know a shifter by that name. Maybe we'll get lucky, and something comes up."

Patrick was starting to worry about how much his uncle was fixating on this. They didn't know what this woman's intentions were. Patrick didn't want to approach her with his uncle slinging threats. It might be better for everyone if Patrick found her first.

Chapter 6

Patrick

"Melody Adams? Why are you trying to find her?" Terrence asked incredulously.

Terrence and his mate were both owl shifters and owned Forest's Edge's only bookstore. It was the third location Patrick checked downtown. By the time he got to Terrence's store, he wasn't expecting much.

"You know her?" He couldn't keep the disbelief from his voice.

"Yeah, of course, with few exceptions, she's in here every Sunday morning as soon as we open. She buys an armload of books and sometimes sells a few back the next week if she didn't like them. She's been coming at least ten years, if not more. Why are you looking for her?" Terrence asked again.

Patrick hadn't come up with a good cover story, so he sputtered. "She dropped her debit card at a friend's house. I found it, and let's just say the host isn't the most reliable of people. I want to make sure it actually gets back to her." As far as lies went, it wasn't a good one. And he wasn't sure Terrence believed it.

"Like I said, she's here every Sunday morning within a half-hour of open, so you can always stop by then."

"Thanks Terrence, you were a big help." He smiled before inclining his head and heading out of the store.

It was Friday. He'd even gotten off work early to ask around about Melody. He wasn't sure how to stop his uncle from doing the same thing until he could corner her on Sunday. Based on the text messages his uncle sent throughout the morning, the older man was fixating on this. Patrick was sure by the end of the day the woman in question would be tied to all kinds of weird Forest's Edge conspiracies. Once Peter started chewing on something he would not let it go, sometimes for years. Just like when five-year-old Archer peed in one of the flower bushes in Uncle Peter's backyard. The next year it did not grow back as well and eventually died. This of course, had nothing to do with Peter over trimming it and everything to do with Archer. It still came up, thirty-two years later.

Deciding to bite the bullet, Patrick pulled out his phone as he stood in the chilly winter air and called his uncle.

"What's going on Patrick? Did you find her?"

"I have a lead. It's solid, so you can stop searching for now. I'm going to ambush her, and I'll let you know what happens."

There was a very loud, menacing growl through the phone. "You're not dealing with her alone. She needs to understand that messing with one bear is messing with the whole clan."

Patrick rolled his eyes. "You don't think I can handle one little shewolf?" He put effort into making his tone sound light.

There was a long pause.

Patrick spoke up again before his uncle could stew too long. "Give me until Monday afternoon, and if I haven't gotten information from her by then, we can go about this your way. Deal?"

There was grumbling Patrick wasn't sure were actual words.

"Fine, you have until Monday at one, at which point I will hunt you down at work, demand your lead, and take care of it myself." Without anything else, his uncle hung up.

Patrick knew he was skating on thin ice. Bear clans were usually just tight family circles. The hierarchy wasn't quite as strong as it would be for a werewolf, but it still wasn't the best idea to tick off his uncle.

But he wasn't sure how else to go about it. Some deep part of him knew he had to find this woman before his uncle did. Not only because Peter would probably be far too aggressive with her, Patrick needed to find her, to protect her from his uncle. He didn't know what was driving his instinct to meet her before his uncle, but Patrick always trusted his instincts. Whatever was going on, he knew she needed Patrick looking out for her. All he needed to do now was wait until Sunday morning. He would get here as soon as the store opened and camp out until Melody made her appearance.

Chapter 7

Melody

Sunday was Melody's favorite day of the week. With how stressed she had been about her brother and stupid cousins and their stupid plot, she really needed this favorite part of her week. She would go to The Nesting Place, sell a couple books, buy a handful more, head over to Morning Kitty, grab an extremely large coffee and just read for an hour or two before taking the mile walk home. She didn't even let Harrison go with her, though he offered several times.

When the charming little bell jingled above the door, a grin split her face and the stress of the week melted from her shoulders. "Good morning, Terrence, good morning Florence, I only have three books to sell back to you today, if that's all right, I just couldn't get into them."

She walked to the middle of the store where Florence beamed at her from behind the counter.

"Good morning honey, it's always so good to see you. Let's see what you got."

Melody grabbed the three books out of The Nesting Place's reusable bag she bought years ago and set them on the counter.

Florence looked at the top book, her eyes wide as she tapped it. "Genuinely surprised you didn't like this one. This is usually right up your alley."

Nodding, Melody looked at the offending book. "It was kind of a slog."

Making a noncommittal noise, Florence checked her out and gave her store credit for the purchases. They chatted a little, just small talk and pleasantries, before Florence waved her off and Melody headed to her favorite section, fantasy. She loved large epic stories in fantastic places. She loved the stretching of the imagination that went along with it.

As she walked down one of the first aisles on the right side of the store, she caught a scent and stopped walking, her body tensed. She knew that smell. But she wasn't sure where she knew it from. It was intoxicating, and part of her wanted to follow it to its source and let it smother her. She took a deep breath again, trying to figure it out. Before she could, a deep male voice rumbled from over her shoulder.

"You're not an easy person to find, Melody Adams."

She swung around, wide-eyed, her heart practically beating out of her chest. Standing this close to him, his scent engulfing her, and her inner wolf howled.

Mate.

Then it clicked where she knew him from, and dread doused the excitement.

"Crap, how did you find me? How do you know who I am?" She forced down the bubbly butterfly feelings. She couldn't afford to be mated to this man.

She watched as shock crossed his face. He sensed it, too. That connection that would be with them forever. And then confusion, as she openly chose to ignore it. He took a step towards her, and she took an even larger step back.

"Why were you in my backyard last week?" His brows were furrowed as he seemed to war with his emotions.

"I—I don't have an answer for you. At least not one you would like." She wasn't sure she could physically lie, at least not outright, to her mate. It was an absolutely terrifying thing to learn as he was standing right in front of her. She could omit things, but not much more.

"Tell me anyway."

Melody swallowed hard as her heart continued to pound in her chest. Her wolf was confused why they weren't just claiming their mate, why they were standing so far away from him when he would clearly be so wonderful to press up against.

"Somebody left something there, and I didn't think it was right to do that." She spoke slowly, choosing each word carefully.

She couldn't say that one of her cousins developed a weird, obsessive grudge against him and somehow intertwined him with the pack hierarchy they wanted to overthrow. Mick left a bottle of poison on the doorstep. When the glass door opened, the bottle would tip and burn the bear shifter's feet. She didn't understand it since shifters healed pretty quickly. Worst-case scenario, he would be out for a week. It was yet another reason why she thought this whole taking over the pack plan was ludicrous.

"You're not going to tell me what it was?" His expression was guarded now, and she missed the confusion.

Shaking her head, she folded her arms across her chest protectively. "I can't. I also can't tell you why, not because I'm not allowed, but because I genuinely don't understand it." She let her disgust show in her voice.

The large, beautiful man in front of her tilted his head and stared at her. She wanted to run her hands through his short red-brown hair. She dug her nails into her arms to stop herself.

"You're not lying." It was a statement. She knew some shifters could scent a lie.

"No, I'm not," she responded carefully.

"Did you know you were my mate when you snuck into my backyard?" There was a tick in his jaw as he asked.

"No, but I am not interested in having a mate." She said it so low and so quiet part of her hoped he couldn't hear her.

But of course he did, because he growled loudly and took a large step towards her. She scrambled back a few more steps. When it became clear he was going to keep moving, she spun around and ran out of the store. She scrambled down the block with no clear destination but knew she just wanted to get away from the large shifter. She could be wrong, but she was pretty sure he was a bear. Bear shifters were large and could best anyone in a fight, but they lumbered.

After several minutes of running, going up and down several blocks, she turned around, relieved she could no longer see him. She knew she would need to weave around town, leaving a decoy trail.

Her chest hurt; she had been able to lie to him after all. Melody knew being involved with that bear shifter would further endanger him, Melody, and Harrison. She couldn't let herself give in to being fated, not when it would be used against them. Bear shifters were very coupley, and she didn't think she could hide that from her cousins and their gang. But now he was looking for her, knew her name and knew they were mated. He was going to keep hunting her down. Tears pricked at her eyes. Why couldn't something have just been easy for once? So much for a relaxing morning.

Chapter 8

Five Days Earlier
Melody

"Thank you for coming with me Mel. I know you want nothing to do with the pack, I appreciate your willingness to see Alpha Sullivan." Harrison said for the third time as they parked in front of the alpha's house.

When she woke that morning, Harrison was already in the living room pacing, trying not to wake her up. When he told her he thought about it all night and decided they needed to go talk to the alpha, she had asked why "we." He responded he wasn't sure he could do it alone and needed her support. She could also provide verification as a second source. But honestly, Melody just couldn't leave her brother to do this by himself.

So now she was in front of the alpha's house, somewhere she never assumed she would be again.

"It's okay Harrison, let's just get this over with." She gave him a smile and squeezed his arm.

They walked up to the front door in silence and Harrison rang the bell. They waited almost a minute before the door cracked open, and the wary, frustrated alpha poked his head out.

"Harrison, Melody what could possibly bring you to my house this early in the morning?"

The alpha owned Murray's, the local tavern with the best fried food in town. It meant he usually didn't get up before one, so eight in the morning was almost cruel.

"Al—Alpha, may we come in and speak to you for a couple minutes please?" Her brother's voice was shaking with nerves, and Melody fought not to wrap her arms around his in comfort. She didn't want to make her brother look weak in front of his alpha.

The alpha snarled before stepping back so they could come in. Once the door shut behind them, he turned to Harrison, folding his arms over his massive chest. "Speak."

Harrison spilled everything about their cousins and everything they overheard at The Watering Hole.

When Harrison finished, the alpha slowly turned his head to Melody. "Is what he's saying true by your account? Is that what you heard?"

She gave a brisk nod. "Yes."

He waited a beat for her to elaborate, and when she didn't, he sighed. "This doesn't give me a lot to go on."

He began tapping several right-hand fingers against his left arm as he thought. The three of them stood in silence for a long stretch. Melody swore it was several minutes before the alpha made a laughing sound in his throat and turned back to Harrison.

"I have an idea, if you're willing. I would like you to help your cousins, they've already reached out to you. I'm not saying I want you to do anything against the wishes of your own conscience or the pack, but if you get enough information about what they have planned and could give me a heads up, I would appreciate it. I understand, though, if you don't wish to be any more involved in this than you already are."

Melody fought her growl, her wolf was equally angry. That this man would dare put Harrison in harm's way made her want to rip his throat out. But she knew better than to do that, so she clinched her jaw and stayed silent.

"I can hang around them, see if I pick anything up. It wouldn't be weird if I just spent time with them as their cousin. But they might think it's weird for me to challenge Melody since she's made such a big deal about them not being in the apartment."

The alpha didn't seem pleased with that answer.

Melody growled deep and low, not able to stop herself now that her brother was tentatively agreeing to this plan. "You're not endangering my brother. I don't know what these morons are planning, but no one is putting Harrison in harm's way."

The alpha's eyes flashed at her, and she swore for a second he was going to launch at her, so she braced for a fight.

Then he sneered, and his muscles relaxed. "I don't intend to endanger anyone. We just need more information so we can plan accordingly. Because if the plan is to overthrow us, there's going to be a lot of bloodshed. Pack wolves don't like coups unless the alpha is a monster. It would cause all sorts of chaos. It is best for the pack if we nip that in the bud."

Melody wanted nothing to do with pack politics, but if the pack was in chaos, it could make problems for everyone else in Forest's Edge, not just the wolves.

Matching the alpha's snarl, she folded her own arms across her chest. "Fine, but he is not doing it alone. I will be there with him, and I say when he's done."

Much to her surprise, the alpha quirked up his eyebrow, and his lips twitched into an almost smile.

"It's probably best for everyone you decided not to be part of the pack. I am not sure a wolf as dominant as you could handle it. I'm not sure we could either."

Melody bristled slightly, even though she agreed with him. She wasn't about to admit it.

"Do we have a deal then?" She held out her hand for him to shake.

The alpha looked from her to Harrison. "Are you okay with her speaking for you?"

Harrison snorted and shrugged. "Yeah, she's never steered me wrong before." He said it with such nonchalance that her heart gave a twinge of affection.

The alpha seemed amused as he turned back to Melody, shaking her hand. "You have yourselves a deal. I want reports from Harrison any time something happens. Preferably, I'd like at least one report a day, even if it's to say you had no communication with them." He gave her hand one last shake before letting go and she nodded.

"All right, we will leave you to get back to sleep." She waited to see if Sullivan responded. When he didn't, she stood and yanked open the door, motioning for Harrison to walk out first.

They stayed silent until they were in the car and driving away.

"You don't have to, you know. Throw yourself into the fray," Harrison muttered.

She snorted. "As if I was going to let you stumble into this mess by yourself. I don't think this is a stable situation. I think they're egging each other on, and you're not safe without backup. And you would've done the same if roles were reversed."

He gave her a large glowing grin. It lit up his face and took years off his age. Melody couldn't help but smile back.

"All right, when I'm on my lunch break today, I'll text them and put out some feelers. Then, we'll go from there."

Melody nodded, knowing things were not going to be so easy and not enjoying the idea of being a spy for groups she never wanted to be involved in. But for her big brother, she'd walk into fire.

Chapter 9

Present Day
Patrick

Patrick stood there in utter shock, mouth open, slack-jawed. His mate just ran from him. She turned tail and bolted from the shop. Not only had he not gotten answers, but he somehow found his mate and she wanted nothing to do with him. Her words had been like a punch to the gut. This was not how this was supposed to go. Fated mates were perfect for each other. The two of them should have embraced. It should have been one of the happiest moments of their lives.

Finally, his growling bear slapped some sense into him, and he bolted after her, taking a huge inhale as he left the shop to decipher which direction she had gone. She already had a sizable lead. Patrick knew she was a wolf, which meant odds were against him catching up with her unless she stopped. His bear roared in his head, pushing him forward at top speed. Wolf shifters had the best sense of smell and were faster than bears. He was at a disadvantage on both fronts.

After several blocks, it became clear she wasn't running in any particular direction but was misdirecting him by doubling back several times. He growled and stopped before he yanked his phone out of his back pocket and called the only person he knew would have any experience with this, any recent experience that is.

"Hello," his big brother Ollie answered cheerfully.

Ollie found his mate two weeks ago, and while she didn't run from him, she was human, so there had been obstacles they had to overcome.

"Ollie, I have a problem," he growled into the phone. His bear was too close to the surface for his voice to sound normal.

"What the hell happened? I can be out of the house in five minutes." There was shuffling in the background.

"It's nothing like that." Patrick took a deep breath before spewing out the lead up to him meeting his mate. Surprisingly and luckily, Ollie had already heard about the weird notes being left at his house.

There were several moments of silence, then his brother had the audacity to start cackling. Patrick yanked the phone away, snarled at it, and waited until his brother composed himself.

"Sorry, I'm sorry. That she ran away is just absolutely hilarious. You're kind of a ladies' man. Not as much as Archer but still, and your mate ran from you. This is something I will never let you live down and will tell all of our siblings."

"That's terribly helpful brother, thank you." His growl deepened. If he didn't calm down soon, he would be fighting for control with his bear. He knew better than to partially shift downtown.

"Okay, okay let's think this through. You know who she is, you know her brother is part of the pack. That means she lives in or around the city. You know she visits the bookstore, and that she escaped on foot. I'm willing to bet that means she lives within three miles of the bookstore. You can walk around the houses and apartment buildings within that radius and see if you smell her scent? It would be tedious, but it might get you closer. If she's in an apartment, at least you know the building. I know that's not the most helpful suggestion, but really that's all I got since the alpha isn't willing to help you."

Growling in frustration, Patrick ran his hand through his hair, probably causing it to stick out in all sorts of directions.

"You're right. At this point, that might be all I have. I appreciate the idea even though it's probably not going to lead anywhere."

"Hey man, look on the bright side, she's a local. She's been there every week for years. That means it'll be hard for her to uproot. So as long as you're keeping your eyes open, you're going to find her eventually. If you don't find her today, we'll gather up the siblings and question the alpha again. Maybe knowing she's your mate will make him more agreeable."

Patrick refrained from commenting that he hadn't found her before this, and they'd both lived there for years. "All right, thanks big brother. I will let you get back to your mate."

"She's teaching me to play cribbage." Ollie sounded absolutely delighted.

Patrick felt a pang of jealousy. He couldn't help his sad smile. "You bunch of nerds. I'll talk to you later."

"Bye," Ollie chuckled before hanging up.

After Patrick slid his phone into his pocket, he proceeded to do as Ollie suggested and took a walk within a mile or two in each direction in a giant circle. After more than an hour, he was so frustrated he finally gave up. There were enough people walking around town that even if he latched onto her scent, he would probably have to be inside the building to get it. And the labyrinthian trail she had left earlier prevented him from getting anything worthwhile. Forcing himself to stay in human form, he stormed back to his truck and headed home.

Chapter 10

Melody

"Well, this is unexpected. Did The Nesting Place not have any books that interested you?" Harrison called over the back of the couch as Melody locked the apartment door behind her.

Not quite sure how to respond, Melody took a deep breath and just stood with her back to the door. Emotions warred within her until everything felt sore and acidic.

"Whoa, what the hell happened Mel?" Harrison stood in front of her, his arms on either of her shoulders in a matter of seconds. His eyes were wide with concern.

"My mate," she croaked out. "I found my mate." The last part was barely a whisper.

Harrison started to grin but saw how devastated she was, and his lips fell.

"Shouldn't that be a good thing? We didn't have the easiest childhood Mel, and you had to do more than your fair share of growing up early. You deserve to find a mate, one who loves and adores you. Are they not a good person?" He rubbed her arms, trying to soothe her but unsure how to do it.

"It's the bear Mack has been obsessing over, you know the one he tried to poison. He cornered me in the bookstore, I don't know how he found me. As soon as we were up close, we both realized what we were to each other, and I bolted." Her eyes became glassy, and she blinked rapidly.

"Oh Mel, I'm so sorry." Harrison pulled her in for a tight hug.

She didn't have to explain to him why the bear being her mate would be disastrous for them. Why accepting him as her mate could cause problems. They tended to think the same way.

"I'm calling the alpha now. We can't keep doing this. You don't deserve to have to put your happiness on hold simply because of our idiot cousins and their little coup. It's none of your business in the first place, you're only stepping in because of me. And I will not compromise your happily ever after for the pack." He let go and walked back towards the couch.

"No, you can't do that. If we quit now, all the work we've been doing the last week will be for nothing. We have to stay the course." Tears began falling from her eyes, and she swiped at them vigorously.

Harrison frowned at her, his expression full of stern, older sibling authority.

"Absolutely not, this ends here."

She dashed over and grabbed his wrist. "No, let's at least see if we can move up the timeline. They were already planning to sketch out the alpha's routine starting tonight, let's see if we can't push things along without them getting suspicious. If we can, we might not need to do this any longer."

Harrison's face hardened, but he gave one nod. "Fine, tonight only, whether we can make things escalate or not, we are done tonight. I am not going to be the reason you can't be with your mate. I'll make some phone calls to the alpha and our cousins, see if I can't stir the pot a bit." He gave her wrist a squeeze, and she let her hand drop.

He strode into his bedroom. Melody didn't follow, trusting her brother to do what they agreed.

Their parents died just after Melody's thirteenth birthday. Since Harrison was eighteen, he fought for custody, not wanting her to be states away with their nearest aunt and uncle. They both worked hard, but she would argue Harrison had a much more uphill battle than she.

As much as she wanted a mate, the guilt in forcing Harrison to live alone after being nearly inseparable for years almost overshadowed it.

Chapter 11

Patrick

"Are we absolutely sure it's a good idea to storm the alpha's house and demand information?" Janet asked from the back seat of Ollie's truck.

Spencer, who was stuck between Janet and Archer, nodded vigorously. "Yeah. Also, I'm not sure why I, the human, am here."

Shifting the truck into park, Ollie turned and raised an eyebrow to their younger brother. "What? The time to question that would have been when we picked you up from your condo."

Shrugging, Spencer looked out the window. "Sure, but at that point, I didn't know what we were doing. Also, it looks like the alpha's leaving his house and getting into that crossover over there."

At Spencer's words, four heads turned. Sure enough, the alpha walked out of his house, Mark with him, and pulled out down the driveway.

"Okay, are we about to stalk the alpha?" Archer waved his arms in a stopping motion expressing how ludicrous he thought the idea was.

Patrick growled at his siblings. "He knows where my mate is and refuses to tell me. So yes, we're to follow the alpha. If for no other reason than I can't just continue to do nothing."

Silence filled the car, several beats later, Ollie started the engine again and slowly followed the alpha at enough of the distance they wouldn't tip them off.

"Well, this is going to be interesting," Janet muttered in the back seat.

No one responded to her, and instead, they drove in silence for more than fifteen minutes.

They started exchanging worried glances once they reached the city limits. Patrick was fairly certain they were heading towards the pack office building. While he didn't know exactly where it was, he knew it existed, and no other shifters were allowed there without invitation. He was probably taking his siblings into a situation they would not be able to back out of, but Patrick knew he couldn't go back, he had no other way of finding Melody unless he continued to stalk the bookstore, and he was fairly certain she wouldn't stick to that routine, at least not for a little while.

"Dammit," came Archer from the back seat as the alpha turned off on a side road. "Don't follow. Keep driving," Archer commanded.

Ollie did as their older brother instructed but slowed way down.

"Park anywhere on the side of the road. We're going to want to walk the rest of the way. I don't think we want the wolves to know we're on their land until absolutely necessary. We can just hope there isn't some sort of pack meeting happening because the whole pack is certainly not going to look kindly on this misadventure."

Patrick's chest grew heavy as Ollie eased the car off the road, and all five of them hopped out. As his heartbeat faster he tried to calm his body down. It was just Sullivan and Mark, Patrick wasn't endangering his family. But even telling himself that didn't seem you calm his nerves.

"Don't worry, I've got you if things hit the fan." Janet whispered to Spencer as they started walking into the small, wooded area in front of them.

Patrick turned around to see Spencer wince. All of his siblings, minus Spencer, were bear shifters. He knew it had been difficult for Spencer to grow up human. He had to rely heavily on his siblings to prevent bullying and help him with the climbing and play that came to bear shifters naturally. But he hadn't wanted his brother to feel left out since all the other siblings were going to confront the alpha. Now he wondered whether he should have just let Spencer feel left out.

They only had to walk for about five minutes before they reached the edge of a clearing where, sure enough, there was a squat four-story office building with a large warehouse next to it. Both the alpha and beta were standing outside the car as if waiting for someone.

"We should probably do this now, before anyone else gets here," came Ollie's suggestion from Patrick's left.

"Yeah, you're right. If anybody wants to hang back here, you can. I'm just gonna jog over to them," Patrick responded.

He didn't wait for a response. Instead, he started a quick jog towards the alpha and beta. They noticed him almost as soon as he stepped into the clearing, and both frowned. The men's eyes scanned past him as his siblings cross into the clearing as well.

When he was a few yards away, he folded his arms and focused all of his attention on the alpha.

"Alpha Sullivan, I need the whereabouts of Melody Adams. She is my mate, and I need to find her before my bear absolutely loses his mind. I know you have her information." Patrick inwardly winced; he was usually much more tactful than this, but his bear was so close to the surface he just didn't have the bandwidth to be polite.

"What? Why didn't you mention this last time we spoke?" The alpha's eyes grew wide as he looked from Patrick to where he presumed his siblings were.

"I didn't know at the time, but I do now."

"Crap," muttered Mark as he rubbed his face. "That explains the angry phone call."

Before Patrick could ask about the phone call, three SUVs pulled in down the road leading to the clearing.

"It's probably best if you guys head out now and we talk about this later." Mark hissed, coming to stand a few feet closer to Patrick.

"Why?" Ollie asked warily.

Ollie made two quick strides so he could stand next to the other man. Their mates were sisters, so Ollie had more interaction with the beta of the Wolfpack than the rest of the siblings did.

"It's a long story. Crap, it's too late now, the doors are opening." As he spoke, he headed back to stand next to the alpha.

Patrick pivoted to the three SUVs that had the wolves so concerned. Two wolves jumped out of the first one. One of them he recognized from the fight at Mark's house about two weeks ago.

"See I told you; I told you those stupid bears were in league with the alpha. He is not making the pack his priority. He's a traitor to our kind." The blonde's expression was fanatical as he pointed to the group of them.

The siblings all moved closer together, making sure they positioned themselves so Spencer was behind the other four.

The second vehicle opened, and another four angry wolf shifters stepped out. Patrick didn't know what the alpha had gotten himself into, but maybe it was best the Roberts family showed up.

The last vehicle's doors opened, and even before she stepped out, Melody's scent hit the air. Patrick was growling before he registered himself doing it.

She stepped out of the back seat of the vehicle with a wolf shifter about her age, who bore a striking resemblance to her. If it hadn't been for that resemblance, Patrick would've felt jealous. But he knew without a doubt this was Melody's brother.

"Please, please tell me your mate isn't the only female wolf in the group of people on crazy pills?" Janet hissed around Archer at Patrick. "No, don't answer that, I could tell by your face. I swear you boys are always getting me into the weirdest situations," she grumbled as she put her hair up in a ponytail, preparing for a fight.

Nerves made Patrick jittery, he didn't like that his mate was going to be in the middle of a fight. He knew the second she saw him—her eyes widened, mouth slid open, and she whispered something he couldn't hear to her brother. The male scanned the group to figure out which bear his sister was talking about.

Not about to let his mate get involved in this, and hopefully none of his siblings either, Patrick strode forward and pushed a snarling shifter aside so he could get to Melody. She seemed frozen in shock, which was fine with him. He could pick her up and walk her right back down the driveway.

Movement beside him drew his attention, but he turned too late as the screaming blonde was right on top of them. Patrick batted him away but not before a sharp pain bloomed in his side. When he looked down, a switchblade was buried in his skin.

Cursing came from behind him, not only from his siblings but from the alpha. Melody shouted in panic. Patrick was starting to feel cold. He looked toward her again and took another step, but it was wobbly. He was vaguely aware of fighting around him, it sounded like more than just his siblings and the wolves from the car, but he couldn't focus. His vision started to go dark around the edges as someone touched the knife. He tried to take another step toward Melody but lost his balance and fell over. He heard Melody scream before everything went dark.

Chapter 12

Melody

Around the time Patrick passed out, two dozen pack members burst from the warehouse to fight this faction trying to overthrow the alpha. Luckily, a medic in the group bee-lined for Patrick when the alpha shouted. The medic beat her to Patrick, as she waded through several idiots to get to them. But once she got there, she knelt down and cradled his head in her lap. The medic glanced at her, and something in her expression must have told him not to argue with her because he simply went back to grappling with the wound in Patrick's side.

He worked in silence for several minutes, slowly pulling out the knife and putting pressure on the wound. The man's shoulders slumped in relief when he smelled the blade.

"It's not silver, it's just regular steel, so he should have this healed within the next twenty hours provided he doesn't bleed out right now."

Tears ran freely down her face, and she let out a sob at the medic's words. Her cousins were going to be locked up, as were the rest of their little gang of idiots. She could actually have a chance at happiness. She couldn't lose it now before it even began. She had so much more to learn about him, she was embarrassed that she only knew his name because two of the shifters shouted it as Mick stabbed him. Patrick knew her name, her weekend routine. He was bull-headed enough to have shown up here, presumably to get information about her from the alpha. She needed him to survive, so she could make it up to him, so she could be as diligent of a mate as he was.

"Stay with me," she whispered while running her hands through his hair.

Once everything subdued and the medic finished treating Patrick, his siblings—or individuals she assumed were his siblings—surrounded them. A large mountain of a man bent down to reach for Patrick, and that's when she snarled and snapped at him.

"No one else is touching him!" Melody snarled over the body of her mate.

He paused mid motion and watched her warily.

"I have to get him into the car. We need to take him home. I can take you home with him." He said the last part quietly and carefully, going out of his way to try to soothe her.

Her wolf snapped and snarled, not wanting anyone near her mate.

"The two of us will sit in the bed of the truck on the ride home. It's not the first or the last time we've done it. You and Patrick can be alone in the backseat." This was from the slightly less bulky brother. He was pointing between him and their sister, who was nodding her agreement.

Melody bit her lip. It went against her instincts to let them help her. While she could probably lift Patrick, bear shifters were dense, and she might not be able to comfortably carry him to the car.

"Fine," was all she could manage, and the word was barely perceivable above the rumble emanating from her throat.

The giant man slowly bent down again, and when she didn't stop him, he gingerly lifted his brother before nudging his chin at the thinnest of the siblings.

"Spencer, you want to get the keys out of my pocket and get the car?"

Spencer nodded before he fished around the brother's left jacket pocket, and when she heard jingling, he stepped back and ran down the driveway.

"We're parked out on the road. We didn't want Sullivan to know we were here until we were ready. Janet, by the way," the sister said as she came to stand on Melody's right. She offered her hand for Melody to shake.

Slowly, Melody shook Janet's hand. "Melody, what are all of you doing here, anyway?"

The other woman snorted. "We were actually here to find you. My brother was determined to interrogate your whereabouts from the alpha, but we stumbled upon you anyway. You want to explain to us why you were part of this little coup, and yet you and that other guy aren't getting in trouble?" The woman lifted an eyebrow at her and looked amused.

Melody glanced over her shoulder to see her brother grinning hugely at her. He waved her off, letting her know she should keep walking and not wait for him. She smiled back and mouthed "Thank you." His grin widened, and he turned back to his alpha.

"We were helping the alpha counter this group's plan to disrupt the hierarchy."

"Ah. Double agents, huh? Nice." Janet bobbed her head as the group continued walking.

Halfway down the driveway, a large dark crew cab truck pulled in front of them. It stopped about six feet away, and Spencer hopped out, leaving the door open. He scrambled around the car then opened the passenger side back door.

The mountain of a man slid Patrick into the back seat.

"You want to get in on the other side so you can prop him up? The cab isn't quite long enough for him to lay down fully," Janet commented as she took a step back, allowing Melody to dash past her.

Giving a weak smile, Melody did just that. As she sat, she rested Patrick's head on her shoulder. It was a weird experience, but just being able to touch him and knowing he was going to be okay had her muscles easing a little.

"Watch the door," Janet called as she shut Melody's door for her.

With Patrick in safely, the rest of the siblings hopped either into the front seat or the truck bed, and they took off back towards the city.

After several minutes of silence, Spencer turned around in the passenger seat and smiled at her. "As you probably heard, I'm Spencer. Our giant driver is Ollie. In the truck bed are Janet and Archer." He looked at her expectantly.

"Melody, and the other man from earlier is my big brother, Harrison."

Spencer smiled weakly. "It's nice to meet you Melody, I wish it had been under better circumstances. I speak on behalf of our mother when I say you are invited and expected to attend Christmas dinner at my parents' house. If it's just you and Harrison, he's invited as well."

Melody blinked at him several times. The last time they had a family holiday of any kind, she was twelve. Secretly, she always wanted a large and close family like this but was nervous and unsure of how to exist in one.

"Thanks," she responded weakly and turned her attention back to the unconscious Patrick on her arm. Slowly, she leaned her head on his and closed her eyes. She didn't have it in her to hold the conversation any longer.

The other man seemed to take the hint, and she heard shuffling as he turned back in his chair.

— — — — — — — —

Once they arrived, Ollie once again opened the door and gingerly lifted Patrick out. All four of his siblings seem to have keys to Patrick's house, as there was a bit of a race to the door before Spencer opened it and stood aside so Ollie could carry Patrick in.

Melody was fully prepared to follow the siblings, but they all stepped off of the concrete slab that made up the front porch and let her go in after Ollie.

"Thank you," she mumbled.

They were a weird kind of processional through the front room and down the hallway on the right back wall. Ollie pushed open the middle of three doors before moving sideways so as not to jar Patrick. Once inside, he softly put his brother on the bed, making sure his feet still dangled off the edge. He straightened and looked a little embarrassed as he made eye contact with Melody.

"Patrick hates the idea of shoes on the bed. He actually doesn't like shoes on the carpet, either. But we just won't mention this to him. Do you want to take off his boots, or should I go ahead and do it since I'm standing here?"

"I'll get it. In fact, I got it from here if you guys want to head back to what you were planning to do with your days. I'll make sure one of us updates you with how he's doing."

The three near the door looked like they were going to protest, but Ollie gave her a large grin before moving around her, patting her on the shoulder as he passed.

"All right then, we'll lock the door behind us." His tone had a finality to it, telling the siblings they weren't going to argue.

Melody waited until she heard the front door open, shut, and the locking mechanism click into place before turning back to Patrick.

He was a gorgeous man. He had the bulk of the bear shifter, but was leaner than his brothers and maybe only a few inches over six feet. He had a sharp jaw and beautiful pale blue eyes she wanted to get lost in.

Shaking herself out of ogling him while he was unconscious, she carefully unlaced his boots and removed them from his feet. Once she had them off, she gingerly maneuvered him into a more comfortable position on the bed and tiptoed out of the room to put both his and her shoes on the shoe rack he had by the front door.

She tiptoed back to the bedroom and slid onto the other side of the bed. She lifted his left arm out so she could snuggle against his side and slide her head over his heart. Not only to be close to him, to have his smell wrapped around her, but to hear his breathing and his heartbeat. After a few moments, the stress of the last few weeks caught up with her, and she dozed by his side.

— — — — — — — —

Melody woke to fingertips brushing up and down her arm. At first, she moaned blissfully at the contact. Then, when she heard a masculine chuckle, she was startled awake before the events of the evening came roaring back to her and she relaxed again.

"How's your side, do you want me to get you some painkillers?" she asked softly as she leaned up and propped her chin on her hands, still laying her hand on his chest so she could look up at his face.

He watched her with sheer joy on his face. "No, but I could think of several other distracting things we could do." The side of his mouth quirked up as he spoke.

"Is that so Mister I-was-stabbed-only-a-few-hours-ago," she answered playfully. "Also, I would prefer you not do that again."

His smile faltered. "I didn't like the idea of you in the middle of a wolf fight."

"I promise you I can more than hold my own."

He shifted his weight like he was about to roll them over, but she put both hands on his chest and scrambled to sit up.

"No, no, no. You are supposed to stay laying down as much as possible for the next—" she looked over at the clock on the bedside table, "—sixteen hours. We're going to abide by the medic's rules."

His brows furrowed, and he grunted in protest.

Laughing, Melody lowered herself so her face was above his own. She wiggled her way as close to the side of his body as she could before leaning in and kissing him hungrily, letting all the worry and hope that ran through her since they found each other flow in the kiss. She pressed her breasts against his chest, and his arm around her waist tightened. His tongue licked at the seam of her lips, and she opened so her tongue could gently play with his. She looped her left leg around his, heat pooled in her core where she pressed it into his hip.

Patrick groaned into her mouth as his right hand came up to her face and gripped the back of her head. The kiss was hungry and frustrated. He stayed still but very clearly telegraphed his need for more. The hand around her waist slowly moved down and wormed its way under her jeans so he could cup her butt cheek.

She moaned as she pressed her breasts against him harder, her body craving more contact, more stimulation. She was careful not to touch his healing cut where she was supporting herself on his chest.

When his other hand made its way down her arm and under her shirt, she whined and Patrick answered with a hungry rumble emanating from his chest. Without moving them apart, he reached above her bra and inside, pulling the cup away and rubbing his thumb across her nipple.

Melody broke the kiss with a gasp. Her swollen lips moved as she panted. His fingers felt so good on her nipple, and she placed her forehead against his.

"Like that do you?" he purred at her.

"Yes!"

The hand on her butt pulled her up and towards him. She let out another needy whine and began slowly grinding against his side.

"That's my very expressive mate," he whispered in her ear. He leaned up and began kissing her neck.

Melody drowned in pleasure, and the hand she was using to prop her up clinched the side of his pillow.

When he let out a hiss of pain, it was like a splash of cold water, and before he could protest, she scrambled off the bed, her breath heaving. Patrick lay with his hurt side in a slight crunch. Melody knew he'd banged his stitches.

"We can't do that, we can't do that right now."

The growl he gave was so loud she was sure it vibrated the bed. Then, he made a motion to roll.

"Absolutely not, Patrick, you stay put. If you don't follow medical orders, I will make you wait longer."

That made him pause. He stopped moving and eyed her suspiciously. They simply stared at each other for several heartbeats before he leaned back on the pillow.

"Fine!" he let out an exasperated sigh, as if she just asked him to fix a garage door.

Melody let out a breath, her shoulders sagged. She was not going to be the reason he didn't heal properly in a timely manner.

"Good, I'll go camp out on the couch. Let me know if you need food or water or something."

"Not happening. You are not leaving my sight; I did after all get stabbed trying to hunt you down. If I'm stuck in bed, you're going to be stuck in bed with me. Even if all we do is play twenty questions."

Rolling her eyes, Melody took several steps towards the bed. "Fine, but no more funny business."

Patrick let out a guttural noise then started unbuckling his belt.

"What did I just say?"

"I am not about to sleep for almost a day in a pair of jeans. They're coming off. You can either help me take them off or I will take them off myself."

Letting out a huff, she moved around the bed and helped him get the jeans off without too much movement. He lifted his arms.

"Shirt too." He smirked at her.

"Really?" She threw her hands on her hips.

"Actually yes. While I enjoy the idea of teasing you, bear shifters run really hot. I will be sweating after several hours sleeping in a shirt."

Melody watched him for several seconds before deciding he was probably telling the truth and, even more slowly and gingerly this time, removed his shirt. "Where do you want the clothing?"

He waved his arm towards the floor. "The floor is fine for now. We can worry about it tomorrow. Or the next day." He winked at her.

Rolling her eyes again, she moved to the other side of the bed before taking off her own pants and shirt.

At the rumble behind her, she turned to see Patrick's expression full of lust. She had to admit, his body was incredible, and she wanted to kiss and lick every inch of it once she was able. She was fairly certain he was thinking the same thing.

"If I lay in the bed next you, are you going to behave yourself?"

He smiled mischievously. "Not one hundred percent. But I promise not to do anything that requires too much movement."

She narrowed her eyes. Patrick was going to be a handful, especially as a patient. It's a good thing for both of them that she was a very dominant wolf.

"If you don't behave, I leave the room, got it?"

"Oh, mate, you are absolutely perfect for me." He chuckled.

When it became clear she wasn't going to move until he answered, he laughed. "Yes, I promise that I will relatively behave. Because if you're lying next to me, I'm going to touch you. But I promise to keep it PG-13."

Mostly satisfied with that response, she lifted the covers and slid underneath them. Wolves didn't run as hot as bears did. Plus, the blanket would be a layer between them that she would probably need to combat his touchy-feely bouts later.

His laugh rumbled through his chest as she sidled up next to him, curling around his side and placing her head on his shoulder, biting back her smile she eyed him with suspicion. This only made him laugh more.

Her heart filled with affection as she lay against him. Having a mate with a playful nature was the one thing she didn't know she needed, and now she had decades to look forward to his teasing. Fate knew exactly what it had been doing. His arm curled around her back, and he moved his fingers up and down in a caress, a comforting gesture. They lay like that for a while before she felt him fall into a doze, his fingers twitching instead of the constant movement, and once she was sure he was asleep, Melody followed, more at peace than she had been in twenty years.

About the Author

Gretchen spawned in the Puget Sound region. After some wandering she returned there and now lives with her husband and the daintiest Rottweiler on the planet. When not drowning herself in coffee, as is custom in the Greater Seattle Area, Gretchen can be found at her day job or sitting at her desk in the home office, flailing her arms as she dictates to her computer.

If you enjoyed this book, please feel free to leave a review on the site of a retailer of your choice. Reviews are always appreciated.

You can find Gretchen at:

Gretchens.b.author@gmail.com
Gretchensb.com
Facebook.com/authorGretchenSB
Tiktok.com/@gretchensb

Turn the page to find out more about Gretchen's other series.

Forest's Edge Series

Forest's Edge doesn't exactly have much opportunity for a shifter to meet their mate, but sometimes their mates are where they least expect them.

Each book has different main characters, though the members of the community keep popping up in other books. The heat level is low, there is some on the page foreplay.

Grizzly Secret
Grizzly Plot
Grizzly Party
Grizzly Theft
Grizzly Kiss

Scent of Home Series

A werewolf knows their mate when they smell them. The smell is said to be like coming home. And though that means something different to everyone it's always unmistakable. While finding one's mate might be easy keeping them is another story.

Each book has different main characters, though the members of the community keep popping up in other books. The heat level is low, with usually just kissing, with more happening off-page.

Alpha's Magical Mate

Kenny's Diner Series

The pay at Kenny's Diner was too good to be true. The night shift seems to bring out everything a little strange. Kathy's pretty sure all the customers are supernatural creatures. But some are a little too hard to explain. It's a good thing this gig pays so well.

Kenny's diner is an episodic series following Kathy, a human server, working at a 24-hour diner that's a hub of supernatural activity.

Don't trust a wolf in a leather vest
Don't get between a dog and his cheese
It May Be Tasty, But it's Still a Bad Idea
You can't see the food through the trees
Have no debt remain outstanding
Not all grandmas are trustworthy
Ignore the rainbow
Let's not make a deal
It's all fun and games until someone loses a pie
Sports are the leading cause of death

Night World Series

These paranormal romances take place in a world with warriors, werecreatures, immortals, and magical practitioners. A rebellious plot may be coming to North America but that isn't stopping fate from putting the Night World inhabitants in the paths of their mates.

Each book has different main characters, though the members of the community keep popping up in other books.

Trigger Warnings: Some light fight scenes, kidnapping, consensual adult scenes.

Lady of the Dead
Viking Sensitivity
A Wolf in Cop's Clothing
Hidden Shifter
Visions Across the Veil

Berman's Wolves Trilogy

While in college an experiment goes horribly wrong and hundreds of students are turned into werewolves. Now years later these werewolves struggle to survive on their own as strange scientists try to take them for experimentation one by one. The more they dig into those scientists, the bigger their problems seem to be. Even their own are keeping secrets and could change everything.

Trigger Warnings: Some mild fight scene.

Berman's Wolves
Berman's Chosen
Berman's Secret
Berman's Origin *(A companion Novella)*

Anthony Hollownton Series

Anthony Hollownton is a workaholic homicide detective. When a case has him stumbling into the supernatural world, he finds it hard to believe. Even when he finds familiar faces. He wants no part of it and they don't want him there either. Yet case after case he's pulled back in.

Trigger Warnings: Some light fight scenes, graphic crime scenes.

Hollownton Homicide
Hollownton Outsiders
Hollownton Legacy
Hollownton Case File *(A companion Novella)*

Jas Bond Series

Jas owns a supernatural antique store he inherited from his mother. Though as a magicless son of the witch he doesn't always have a lot in common with his customers. All Jas wants is to live a quiet life with Bailey his goofy Rottweiler and run the store. But the characters who come into his shop keep yanking him back into trouble.

Trigger Warnings: Some light fight scenes.

Green Goo Goblin
Spectacle Stealing Supernatural
Book Burgling Blood Magic
Antique Absconding Arsonist
Property Pilfering Pariah

Lantern Lake Series

The holiday season is a big one for lantern Lake. Though the lake is surrounded by three small towns their holiday festival is something people come to see from all over the state. Not only does winter bring that holiday festival but it usually brings love along with it.

Each book has different main characters, though the members of the community keep popping up in other books. The heat level is low, with usually just kissing.

Pizza Pockets and Puppy Love
A flurry of Feelings
Teacher's Crush
Pugs and Peppermint Sticks
Moving Home for the Holidays
Mayor May Not
Building a Holiday Miracle

Made in the USA
Columbia, SC
17 November 2024